The Littlest DINOSAUR and the Naughty Rock

MICHAEL FOREMAN

Written by Camilla Reid

BLOOMSBURY

LONDON BERLIN NEW YORK

The littlest dinosaur was feeling out of sorts.
He didn't know why, but he was in a **bad mood**.

He went to look for Father Dinosaur.
'Dad will cheer me up with one of his games,' said
the littlest dinosaur.

Father Dinosaur was having a quiet snooze.
'Play with me, Dad!' demanded the littlest dinosaur.
'Hmm,' smiled Father Dinosaur, slowly opening one eye.
'I might if you ask **nicely**.'

The littlest dinosaur **stamped** his tiny foot.
'But I just need you to play with me to make me HAPPY!'
'I see.' Father Dinosaur frowned. 'Well, if that's the way
you're going to behave, I'm not going to talk to you at all.'

And with that, he turned over and went back to sleep.
'Baaah!' said the littlest dinosaur, and he marched off
to look for his brothers and sisters.

They were in the meadow, playing leapfrog.
'Can I join in?' asked the littlest dinosaur.

'You're too small for this game,' explained his eldest sister. 'Try to find someone your own size to play with.'
'No!' yelled the littlest dinosaur. 'I want to be with you.'
'Well, we're not going to play with you if you **shout** at us!' And his brothers and sisters ran off.

The littlest dinosaur felt grumpier than ever. He went home to find Mother Dinosaur.

'Hello, dear,' she said, as he appeared round the corner. 'Would you like some lunch? It's fern leaves – delicious!'

The littlest dinosaur had been looking forward to **palm leaves** – he didn't feel like eating **fern leaves** at all. He picked up the pile of crisp green shoots and threw them into a very muddy puddle.

This time it was Mother Dinosaur's turn to be cross. 'Right!' she snapped. 'That's it. You've been rude to your father, you've shouted at your brothers and sisters and now you've ruined your meal. Go and sit on the naughty rock until you've calmed down and can behave properly.'

The littlest dinosaur had never sat on the naughty rock before and he didn't like it one little bit. It was cold and hard and uncomfortable, and the other dinosaurs could see him up there, all by himself. He felt terribly ashamed.

A big, wet tear rolled down his cheek.

But then, an extremely strange thing happened. Slowly, the rock began to move! First to one side, and then to the other, the rock was **rocking**. A moment later, a funny wrinkly head appeared and looked up at the littlest dinosaur.

'May I ask what you are doing?' said the head.

'You're the naughty rock,' sniffed the littlest dinosaur. 'I'm sitting on you because I've been a **very naughty dinosaur**.'

'I most certainly am not the naughty rock!' said the head
indignantly. 'I am a **giant tortoise** and I'd rather you didn't
sit on me . . . Oh dear. You're not a happy little chap, are you?'

'No,' sobbed the littlest dinosaur. 'I'm not. I've been grumpy and rude and no one likes me any more.'

'Don't worry,' said the tortoise. 'You know, everyone has bad days now and again. The trick is to remember to say please and thank you – then people will **want** to be kind to you.'

'Oh, I **see**,' said the littlest dinosaur, brightening a bit. 'Now, off you go and say sorry. I'm sure everyone will be happy to see you.'

So, feeling very much better, the littlest dinosaur trotted away.

The giant tortoise was right, of course.

As soon as the littlest dinosaur apologised to his family, they forgave him and had a big kiss and a cuddle.

And then they went out for a game of hide-and-seek,
which was the littlest dinosaur's most favourite game of all.

The next day, the littlest dinosaur went to find the giant tortoise.

'Hello, young man,' said the tortoise. 'I hope you haven't come
to sit on me again. I don't think either of us wants that, do we?'

'No,' giggled the littlest dinosaur, 'we don't! Actually,
I've taken your advice and everyone **has** been very
nice to me. So I've come to say . . .

THANK YOU!'

Then the littlest dinosaur gave the giant tortoise a kiss on his great big wrinkly nose.

'You're most welcome,' said the giant tortoise.